THE
GREAT CASTLE OF
MARSHMANGLE

written by Malachy Doyle

with illustrations by Paul Hess

Ⓐ

Andersen Press
London

The day I was five I went to the fair.
I met my Grandaddy for the very first time.
He's the funniest wee man you've ever seen.

He had a yellow top hat on,
A plum-coloured jacket,
Rainbow breeches,
Polka dot socks,
Bright silver boots,
And a white, white beard
reaching all the way down
to the golden buckle on his belt.

"Hello, young man," said he. "Would you like
to come and stay with me in the Great Castle
of Marshmangle for the night?"
I looked at Mummy and she was smiling.
"Yes, sir," said I. "I'd like it very much."

Up a high hill we walked and down into a low valley,
Off the hard road and onto the soft,
Till we came to a place where the trees were growing
Both sides of the lane and over the top.
Through the tunnel and out of the tunnel we went,
Till the path turned left and we came to a clearing.

There in front of us was a little thatched cottage.
"What do you call that, young man?" said my Grandaddy.
"How do you mean, sir?" said I.
"Well, what sort of a name would you give to that thing
in front of you?"
"Oh, the house, or the home, or whatever you say, sir," said I.
"You wouldn't be right there," said he, laughing.
"Sure, that's the Great Castle of Marshmangle."

He took a big key out of his pocket,
Opened the door, went in and threw some
wood on the fire.
"And what would you call this, young man?"
said he.
"That's the flame, or the fire, or whatever you
say, sir," said I.
"Indeed not," said he. "It's Smoulderglow."

The next thing a cat came in and stretched out by the fire.
"So what about that wee scrap?" said my Grandaddy.
"What would you call her?"

"Sure she's a kitten, a cat, or whatever you say, sir,"
said I, stroking her head.
"No, no," he said. "That's Pickpocket."

"Well if nothing around here has a name that I know," said I,
"What do I call you, sir?"
"Oh, my name's Hickory Horseradish," said he.
And he picked up the kettle to make some tea.
"What's this coming out of the tap, young man?" said he.
"It's the water, the rain, or whatever you say, sir," said I.
"Not at all," said he. "Soggadrop, that's what it is."

He took off his silver boots,
Tired of walking the whole day long.
"Now what would you call these, young man?"
"Your wellies, your waders, whatever you say,
sir," said I, laughing.
"Not a bit of it," said he. "They're my
Sandcastle Stompers."

"And what about this?" he said,
Knocking the dust off his topper.
"Your helmet, your hat, or whatever you say,
sir."
"Wrong again," said he.
"It's my Brainbox Banana."

"Now," he said, "while we wait for our supper,
I'll show you where to sleep."
"So what would you call this, then?" said he on the way up.
"The steps, or the stairs, or whatever you say, sir."
"Ah no," he said. "It's the Wooden Hill."

He threw open the door at the top of the stairs
To show me my lovely wee bed.
"And what would you call that, young man,"
said he.
"It's the bed, or the bunk, or whatever you say,
sir," said I.
"It's not, indeed," said he. "Sure, it's the
Fortywink Cockpit."

We ate our supper, milked the cow,
Locked the house and went off to sleep.

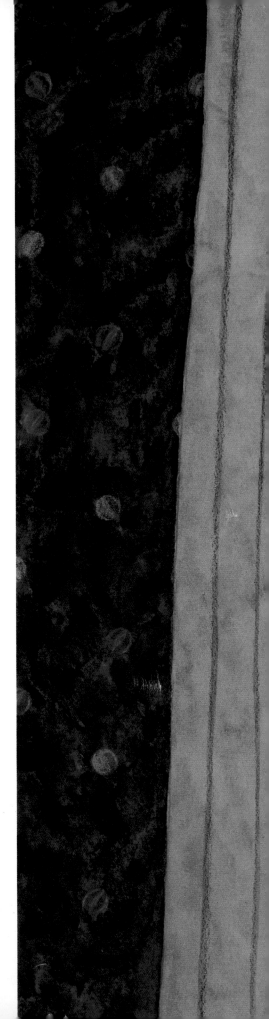

In the middle of the night
I crept down for a drink,
And saw a terrible thing.

I ran to his door. I knocked and knocked.
"What's wrong, young man?" said he.
"Hickory Horseradish!" said I,
"Rise up from your Fortywink Cockpit,
Put on your Sandcastle Stompers and your
Brainbox Banana,
And come down the Wooden Hill!
Pickpocket's got a Smoulderglow on his tail,
And if we don't get some Soggadrop quick
The Great Castle of Marshmangle will be
burnt to the ground!

So out he flies from his Fortywink Cockpit,
Springs into his Sandcastle Stompers,
Bangs his Brainbox Banana on his head,

And down the Wooden Hill as fast as his feet
will carry him.
Sure enough, there's poor wee Pickpocket
Running in rings around the room, shrieking.

Hickory Horseradish grabs a jug of Soggadrop,
And pours it over Pickpocket's tail.

With a shishing and a shushing the Smoulderglow goes out
And the Great Castle of Marshmangle is saved.

The next morning it's my Mummy's turn to come knocking
on the door.
"How did you like staying in the Great Castle of Marshmangle?"
she said, smiling. "I bet it's quiet compared to the town."
"Oh, not so quiet," said I. "Not so quiet at all. Can I come
and stay with my Grandaddy again?"
Mummy looked at Hickory and Hickory looked at me.
"Yes, Michael," they said together. "You can, indeed."

For Hannah – M.D.

Text copyright © 1999 by Malachy Doyle
Illustrations copyright © 1999 by Paul Hess
The rights of Malachy Doyle and Paul Hess to be identified as the author and illustrator
of this work have been asserted by them in accordance with the Copyright, Designs and Patents Act, 1988.
First published in Great Britain in 1999 by Andersen Press Ltd., 20 Vauxhall Bridge Road, London SW1V 2SA.
Published in Australia by Random House Australia Pty., 20 Alfred Street, Milsons Point, Sydney, NSW 2061.
All rights reserved.
Colour separated in Italy by Fotoriproduzione Grafiche, Verona.
Printed and bound in Italy by Grafiche AZ, Verona.

10   9   8   7   6   5   4   3   2   1

British Library Cataloguing in Publication Data available.

ISBN 0 86264 792 4

This book has been printed on acid-free paper